P9-CCV-320

STAR WARS

C-3PO DOES **NOT** LIKE SAND!

Written by
Caitlin Kennedy

Illustrated by
Brian Kesinger

To Jenny, my love across the stars
—B. K.

Printed in the United States of America

First Edition, June 2019

1 3 5 7 9 10 8 6 4 2

Library of Congress Control Number on file

FAC-038091-19116

ISBN 978-1-368-04346-5

Visit the official *Star Wars* website at: www.starwars.com.

LUCASFILM PRESS

LOS ANGELES · NEW YORK

SUSTAINABLE FORESTRY INITIATIVE Certified Sourcing www.sfiprogram.org SFI-00993
Logo Applies to Text Stock Only

A long time ago in a galaxy far, far away. . . .

Goodness, gracious me, have we really returned to this *dreadful* place?

BOOP BEEP?

Yes, I said dreadful, and I *meant* it.
Tatooine is the *last* place I'd like to be!

Let's scan the planet and then get back to the Resistance as soon as possible.
BEO BWOOP BWAP!

No, BB-8, we're not here to have *fun*.

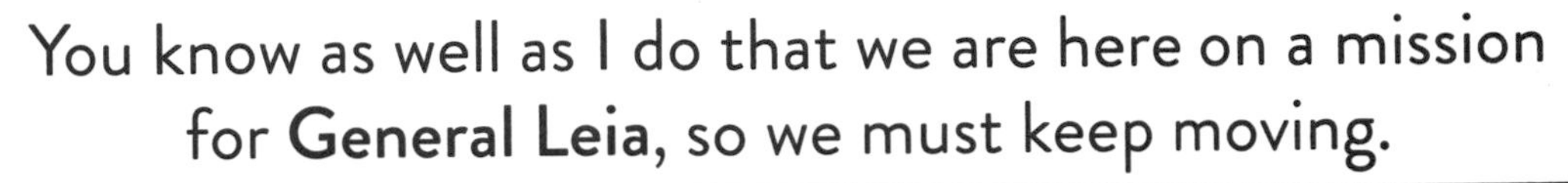
You know as well as I do that we are here on a mission for **General Leia**, so we must keep moving.

But, oh, this *heat*, and all this **SAND**! We seem to be *made* to suffer!
BEEP BOOP BWAP?

Yes, *sand*. The very stuff you've been rolling across, you silly sack of gears.
It is really quite terrible for my circuits, and—
Oh, BB-8, do stop playing with that ronto!

SSLLLUUURRRP

We are here to *work*, you two.
BEO BOP BEEP BOOP BWAP.

What do you mean your "best adventures" have happened on desert planets? Of all the ridiculous things to say!
Don't listen to him, BB-8. He's clearly malfunctioning.
BEE—BO, BOO BEE BA!

Oh, yes, the *girl* . . .
Rey.

Yes, we all know she rescued
you from the dunes on Jakku.
You needn't act it out.

Oh, this horrible sand! It's *everywhere*, and I simply cannot stand it. Not one single bit!

And neither should you two droids if you have half a logic circuit. Now, let's keep moving.
RRROOO
BEEP BIP BWEEP?

I don't know what that sound is, R2, but we're not going *that* way.

We're going *this* way, because this is the way we should go.

General Leia asked me, *personally*, to collect data for her, and a protocol droid would never . . .

OOOM! S

REEEEEE

R2?
BB-8?

VROOOO
Where *are* those silly droids?
And what is that racket?
I don't know what all this trouble is about, but I'm sure it must be R2's fault. . . .

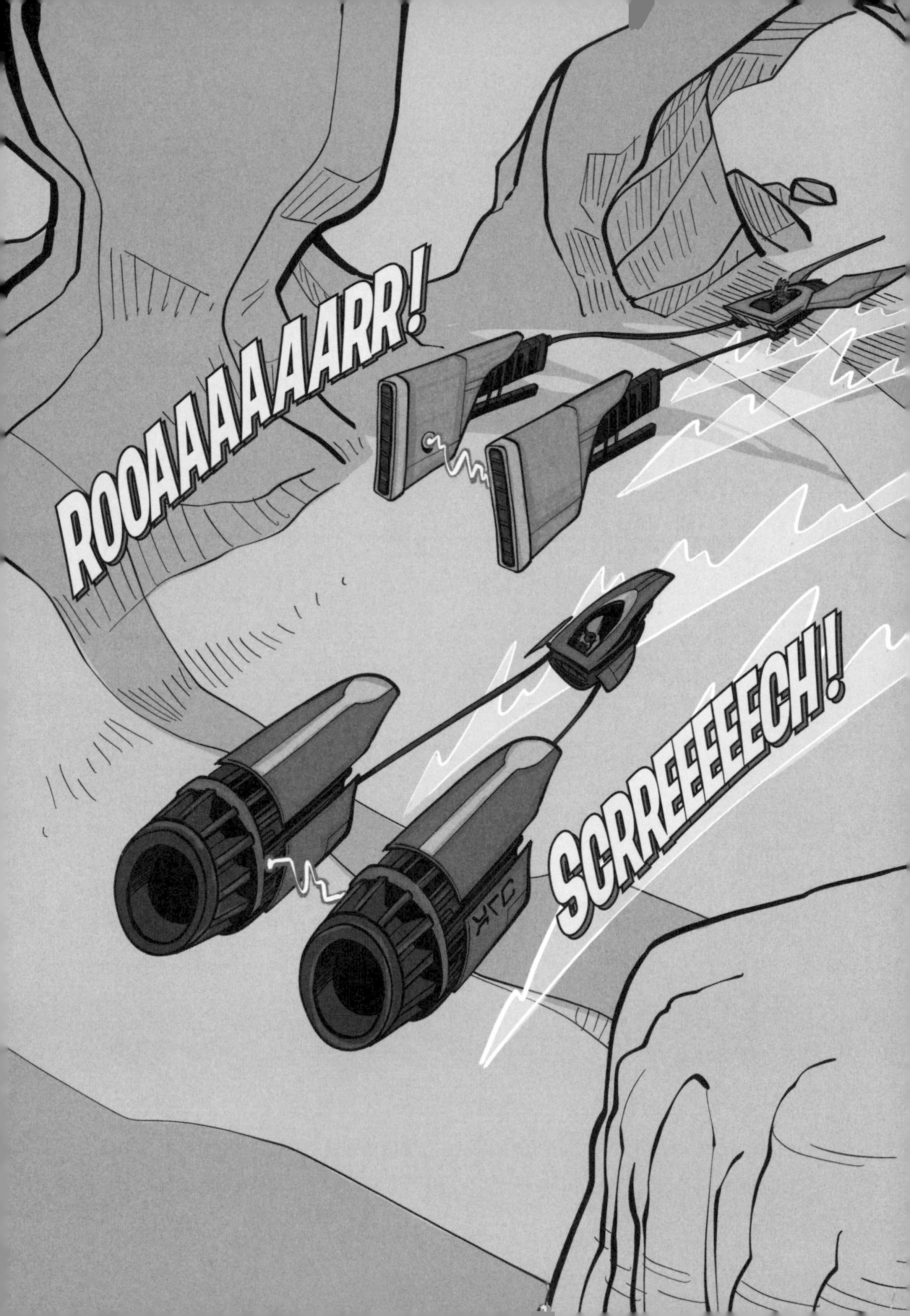
ROOAAAAARR!
SCRREEEEECH!

VRROOOOMM!

SCA-BLAAAMM!
CRROOOOOSSH!

BWEEEEP!
Yes, yes, I can imagine it *was* fun to watch. But we haven't time for podraces.
BWOP.

You watch your language, R2! How General Leia puts up with you is a complete mystery to me.

No, BB-8, come back!
Where does he think he's going?

Now look what you've done, R2. You've lost poor BB-8.
That little round droid *needs* us.
Do you see him anywhere?
BWIP BAPP-BAPP BWOOP.

Playing *tag*? Is that what you said?
Oh, dear. BB-8, come along! Quickly!

BWOOP BWEEP?

No, BB-8, Jawas are not your *friends*. Next you'll be saying you want to play with Tusken Raiders!
Come, come. We have to stay focused on our mission.

Utinni!
ZZZAP!

Now, if my calculations are correct, we should be approaching the . . .

I've just about had enough of you two!
We don't have time for this!

BWEEP BA-BWIP?
No, not even time for sand banthas.
Really, BB-8. Where *do* you come up with these things?

Stop fussing around in that dreadful stuff. You've gotten some in my eye!
BOOP BEEP BEEP BWAP.

Oh, R2! It doesn’t matter that he has forgotten the horns!

I do not like *sand* and I do not like *sand banthas* and this is a waste of our time!
BEEP BOOP BWEEP BAP?

What do you mean, "What about a real bantha?"

Oh, my! No, no, no.
No, thank you, Mr. Bantha.
We will just continue on our way and you can do the same.

Now, really, you are *entirely* too close!
Please, if you would be so kind as to just move along . . .
BOOP BEEP BOOP.

How do *you* know he wants a hug? You don't speak bantha. *I* don't even speak bantha!

Oh, dear, we're doomed!

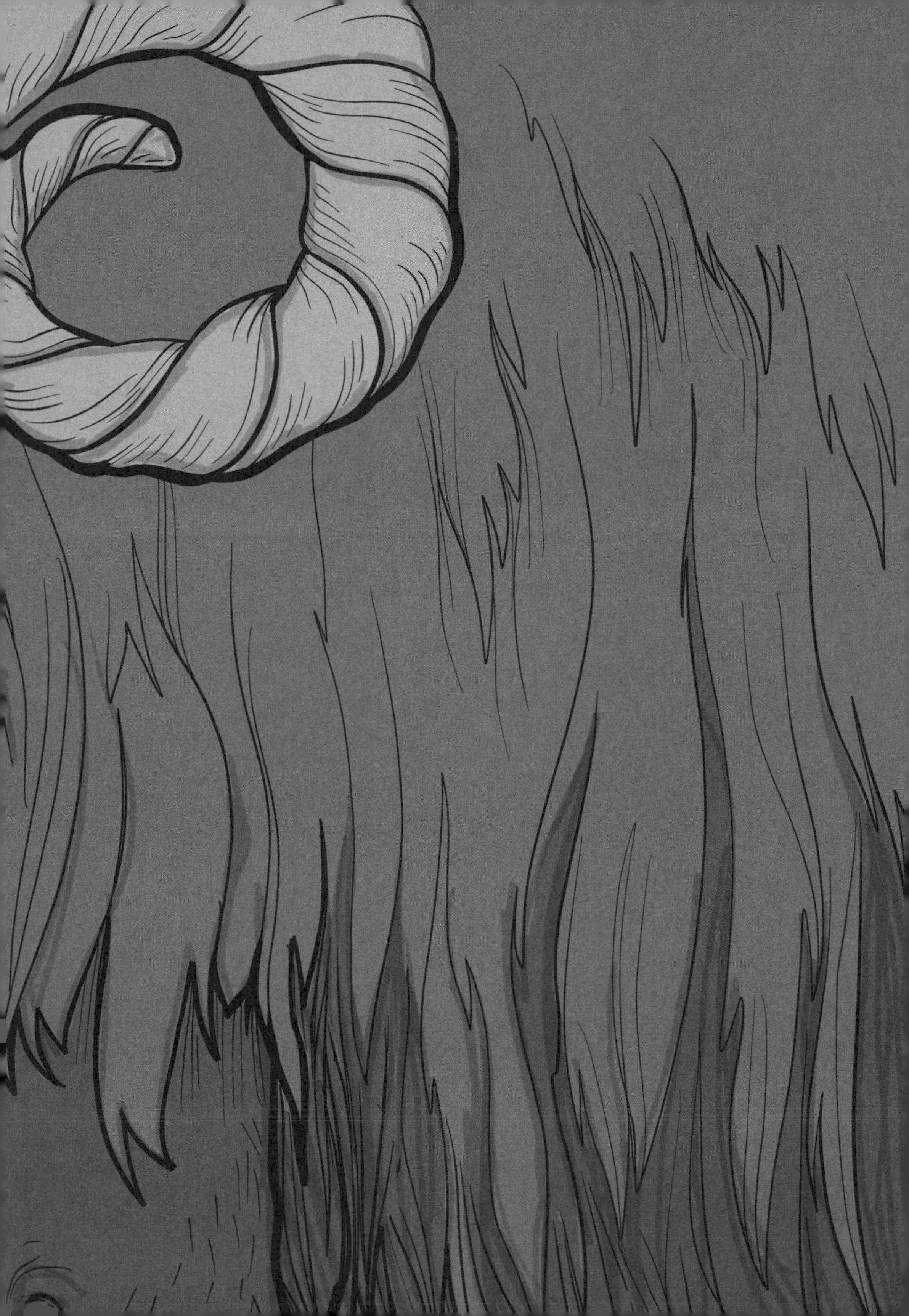

Ooohhh, that smelly brute!
Of all the most unpleasant things!

BWEEP BOP BWEEP BIP?

No, we cannot *keep* him, BB-8!

THAT IS IT!
First sand, now bantha fur.
I HAVE HAD ENOUGH OF ALL THIS!

Thank the Maker!
We've made it back to the ship!
The first thing I'm going to do is take a nice long oil bath to clean off all this terrible sand!
BEEP BOOP BWEEP BAP?

You be quiet, R2!
Look, you're bringing half the desert with you! Who is going to clean all this up?
Not *me*, that's for sure. How glad I am that this mission is over. . . .

If I never see sand again, I'll be the happiest droid in the galaxy.